famished

anna vaught

Influx Press
London

Published by Influx Press
The Greenhouse
49 Green Lanes, London, N16 9BU
www.influxpress.com / @InfluxPress
All rights reserved.
© Anna Vaught, 2020

First edition 2020. Printed and bound in the UK by TJ International.

Paperback ISBN: 9781910312490
Ebook ISBN: 9781910312506

Editor: Gary Budden
Copyeditor: Ella Chappell
Proofreader: Dan Coxon
Cover design: Vince Haig
Interior design: Vince Haig

contents

cave venus et stellas

'Were the succession of stars endless, then the background
of the sky would present us a uniform luminosity.'

Edgar Allan Poe, *Eureka*

It is a strange place; a cold street, in which the temperature seems to drop as you round the corner. You feel the breeze cut into you; sometimes you think you must have imagined it, but no: there it is again. A street that looks the same as the last but also inescapably, irresistibly different.

The young man, lean and callow, has been called upon to work for the shadowy residents of this street. There, every day, post is delivered, collected from doormats, papers from drives and houses and gardens that are maintained in pristine condition. And yet, we see no one, telling ourselves only that the street's inhabitants must keep rather bohemian hours.

So, the young man, a fine carpenter it is said, is called to the fifth house on the street, a high house like all the others, with imposing gables and a tall, tall chimney stack. He rings the bell and a lady answers, ivory and willowy, with intense blue eyes. She sees him start just a little, as one does when confronted with flagrant beauty. 'Won't you come in? So much to do.'

All the time she sips from a little cup. *Sip, sip*. He averts his eyes from her cherry lips. Inside the house, it is a world away from the modern suburban street, all billowing drapes, commodious cabinets of dainty phials and bottles, Venetian mirrors and candelabra. And little cups; so many little cups on narrow shelves. Like the one she carries: *sip, sip*. With fluted saucers, Japanese and Chinese designs, lacquer work. His eye is drawn everywhere all at once and she senses this.

'Yes: I am quite a collector, as you see.'

'Well, I'm wondering, Miss – is it Miss? – which jobs you need doing?'

'Ah, yes, but first, won't you have some tea? Come through. And you may use my first name: *Stella*. Oh, beware of the step there. The step down. Beware, won't you?'

There is a tiny flutter in his heart for the unusual patina of her syntax.

The kitchen is through the long narrow hallway with its intricate pattern of hexagonal tiles. Over the step – do you beware? – and there he is, in a room with a vast azure ceiling, upon which are painted many tiny gold stars. He would have thought it exquisite, had it not already begun to make him dizzy. On the floor he thinks, counting quickly, that he sees aureate stars, limned with a pretty language he does not know.

So exquisite.

But she distracts his gaze and boils water in an old-fashioned urn (strange, he thinks, why no kettle?); rather too much for tea for two. She makes tea in a lovely, highly polished silver pot – again it seems disproportionately large. They drink, though it is sour.

Sip sip.

'I need more shelves. Long, thin shelves for my display. I am such a magpie, as you saw. And shallow cabinets for the walls. As you might see in an old-fashioned apothecary. For my pharmacopoeia. Ha! But not so deep and, you know, with drawers. Can you picture what I mean?'

Yes, for the first. That shouldn't be hard. But her second request would be more difficult. He is too shy to say he cannot translate all her words. As he drinks his tea, he feels he wants to please her, so he agrees to start all work the next day. His other commitments tell him he should wait, but there is something about this lady – and she amuses him too, he thinks as he drinks the tea from her little cups.

—⁂—

Next day he begins and, in a day, the narrow shelves are cut and fitted for the bare little anteroom off the kitchen. 'This will be my dining room,' she says. 'You are decorating it for me.'

He drinks more of her tea, finds his manners are more refined in front of her, *sip, sip,* and even picks at dainty sandwiches she makes him, paring their edges with his incisors, as she does, behind those cherry lips.

He begins work on the cabinets. The work flows from him; some of his best work to date. Invisible joints and gloriously conceived design. He has surprised himself. But then, standing back from the room, as it begins to come to life with its first fittings, he feels suddenly tired, and this she sees.

'Come and sit down. In the kitchen. Do beware the step, again.'

She looks more beautiful than ever today, he thinks. But she's his customer, so he must not say it aloud, though to think he might thrills him. And look at her milk-white tapering fingers; ancient, young. Long nails. 'Yes, I had better. I had better sit.' He is not himself, while her beauty swirls and fizzes stars.

He sits, closes his eyes for a moment to rest. He feels worse. Looking up at the ceiling and so at the fine golden stars, he becomes dizzier, then blithe, finally hollow. His extinction is deeply pleasurable, until he sees and remembers no more. 'Orris root and henbane, my darling,' she says, stroking his cadaver and removing the cup and saucer from the still-warm hand. And now. The umbrageous inhabitants of the rest of the houses in the street come through interconnecting doors – they are corporeal, after all – and they feast and they drink him dry from the little fluted cups as they sit under the stars. And what they cannot digest, they grind for their medicines and potions, even a dainty cosmetic for the ghostly powder-pallor of their complexions, and this they place in the shallow apothecaries' drawers. Their pharmacopoeia. Ha! And thus, they retreat to their own homes and the lady with the lovely blue eyes is alone. Until, that is, she crosses her hall to the next visitor who will come to her, while she is floating, as she will be, across the fine, encaustic tiles. And across the pretty pentangles, with the Latin inscription which the carpenter did not know how to read: 'Cave Venus et Stellas'.

It is a strange place; a cold street, in which the temperature seems to drop as you round the corner. You feel the breeze cut into you; sometimes you think you must have imagined it, but no: there it is again. A street that looks the same as the last but inescapably, irresistibly different.

feasting; fasting

'You will feel no pain, my darling.'

Angela Carter, 'The Lady of the House of Love'

The grand old house, in the sleepy French village, is tall and dusty looking. Once, it must have been vibrant, but now, bindweed curls around it and ivy reclaims the windows and the stone of the walls. It must be hard for the quiet inhabitants to see out. Sometimes there is post for the house, and the post boy makes a swift passage towards the door because the house alarms him. There is a housekeeper, a rufous old crone who will not give you the time of day, and, curiously, a gardener – though he never tends to the front gardens, so fallen into disrepair they are. The villagers wonder whether there are comely, well-tended lawns and pretty herbals to the rear of the house.

It is said that a lady lives at the house; some say two sisters, and that they never need company. Some say it is merely a mausoleum, kept up for love by last testament of star-crossed, liverish lovers. Well here is a canard truth: this is a house of shadowy presences, a place where melancholy hangs thick in the air. And at night, sometimes – in summer, when the top windows of the house are open – one hears music, from a curious assortment of instruments: flute, cello, but also mandolin and dulcimer. An inhabitant of the village making his way home could be stopped in his tracks because the music is so extraordinarily beguiling. And even so it sends a shiver up the spine which is not so pleasant. A death song you're frightened you might not resist. A tune to lead you up the tenebrous spiral staircase of the self.

But today is different. People do not come and go readily in this village, yet a new person has come, from the city, and he wants to enquire about the tall, grand house. He thinks he might like to buy it: a retreat. It has tremendous fiscal potential and he knows excellent architects and designers in Paris, where he lives now. He is bold, so he knocks at the door and it is answered. One rumour, one canard truth. Two women come to the door, so similar facially it is immediately clear that they are sisters. They are not beautiful, but they are arresting – I am sure you know the quality of which I speak: striking and sensual women, with poise and grace; exquisite manners, too. They seem pleased to see him and – he is surprised to entertain this peculiar thought for a moment – as if they knew he were coming. But when a man is so confident, he does not notice that a shadow should be cast on a fine day, or a reflection shown in silvery glass. Our understanding is infirm: our known world is only a beginning.

So, more fool him, as the ladies' footsteps make no fall.

Over tea and dainty cakes, he explains to them what he is looking for. They are clearly amused by something but do not elaborate. And to his sure delight (*he was right; he was right: he is an imposing man, yes, yes*) they indicate quite clearly that, indeed, they were thinking of releasing the house, this fine château, of perhaps finding somewhere smaller because the great house is too much to manage and they realise parts of it are in a poor state of repair. (*Yes yes; too much for these women; what perspicacity he has*, he thinks.) They tell him that they will be in touch, that they have a solicitor in Paris who attends to matters of estate and finance for them, and so the visitor takes his leave. The women watch him and see that even his footsteps brag.

Thus, he confidently waits and, sure enough, within weeks he hears from them again. A sum is agreed and the solicitors are instructed. Within two months, he is in the house, commanding the removal of dust and grime and revealing the lovely home he perceives under the crumbling plaster and neglect. He has a lady in Paris, and she becomes his wife. So taken with the enriched house is he that he decides to move from Paris and he begins to stow his acquisitions there, in the new place: boxes, trunks, his near-priceless things – a Roman marble cuirassed bust bought by haughty hands, coins dripping through those hands like water. He is a collector. It is a fair trip from burnished splendour and other chattels in Saint Germain-des-Prés, but he thinks he can make the journey once or twice a week to conduct his business. *I am building a 7th arrondissement here, in this village. I shall expand and purchase a village*, he jokes to himself. His new wife will be happy with that; with such increase. He agrees that the rufous crone and the old

15

gardener will attend, until further notice. He has purchased them, too. During the times of absence, his new wife is left lonely at home, but she will manage and accommodate.

They, the crone and the gardener, will convene with her appropriately. And it is done.

But the new wife sits and sulks; she loathes her abode because he carved it. And loathes her new husband. Heavy tread. Greedy pawing. She wishes to carve into him; to see if he's still so vainglorious when layers of flesh are sliced through like velvet coat incarnadine. Sees herself consumed within these layers. In time she rails aloud. After this, there is nowhere she can go. She is not of independent means. To return to her parents would be an abominable shame, though she was never loved since cradle days. Her tears are insistent, though there is faint comfort in the two old retainers who bring handkerchief and posset for her tears. She says that her life is over, and the hearts of the two soften daily, for her words to them are kind.

Still, for days and days she cries, until she pushes the marble from its pedestal and howls into the warm night as the near-priceless effigy tumbles. Oh, for nakedness and for something, anything: annihilation, love, a horror to make me feel alive! She tears at her gown. What is this? Her eyes violet, livid.

Call, croon and summon. Sisters. Sister. She is awake to it, the back of her hand smoothed and tingling.

And so, they come to her.

The two sisters secreted in the deeper recesses of darkness until they saw a purpose. One day, the rufous old crone and gardener will go the same way, and they look forward to this gentle extirpation. Like the sisters, they will never leave this alive house: a living, breathing organism and the sisters, hungry for dim, mysterious life, part of its dark heart. The house may be trimmed and tidied and made pretty but, underneath, it will not change. And so the young wife is dissolved to the marvellous gloaming; her corporeal life prophesies nothing for her. So. And when her husband, upstart from Paris, comes back, he will not find her. And into a maw will he go too. But *different, different!*

For the new wife, claiming will be kind.

A life lived without love, she now finds company and subtle delight. And the satisfaction of knowing that his, her husband's, will not be a quiet taking. And all those – they are legion – who live in the wings of the house and in the fine rear garden will play their music, jangle the gold of our upstart, kiss the new wife and she them, and do what cruel things they must, laughing, surviving, mouthing hard; hot. You could hear them if you went to this village on a summer night when the music is played, where strangeness is a winged thing, brushing your arm in aliform delicacy, and going dark. But see! Lying in a grand first-floor room are the myriad pieces of a cuirassed Roman bust, a jigsaw never done, though cusped by an unseen laugh.

what he choked on

'People who deny the existence of dragons are often eaten
by dragons. From within.'

Ursula K. Le Guin, *The Wave in the Mind*

It was a cosy little place; novel, *Thai Tapas* they called it.
Which meant small portions of Thai food. And the boy
was excited to go in. But just a little scared, too. He'd never
tried Thai food and thought tapas sounded Spanish and,
he recalled now, all his experience of Spanish food was an
omelette heavy with vegetables and a slice of Manchego
cheese that his turophile grandmother had made him try
with olives. The hybrid seemed mysterious, if not just a
touch menacing.

At Grandmother's house, as the affineur swept forward
bearing an old wooden board with little bits on it, he'd
worried. That was because Grandmother expected him to
try and he didn't always want to; but he didn't want to
disappoint her. The olives he'd liked. The cheese tasted

of saddle and the hair of beasts in heat. He shuddered at this memory. Now how, he wondered, have they combined such things with Thai food? Thai food, Mother had explained, was *sweet and sour, and you couldn't taste the anchovies in the fish sauce, but you did get whacked by a deep, savoury flavour. And there was a smack of chillies. It was a flavour which could quickly become addictive.* On, she went, as mothers do, about *the aniseed taste of Thai basil and the lovely lemony smack* you got too. And the boy's anxiety began, surely and slowly, to increase.

Hot beasts in heat.

Crumbly white cheese.

Some sort of omelette.

Lemony things that smacked you, and things that could be addictive.

Aniseed. Wasn't that like liquorice?

Sweet. Sour. A sauce made of old fish, but they'd disguised the fish because you could always taste fish and surely that was not trustworthy. It was a deception. What else was in there that added flavour, but which you couldn't clearly identify? Other (slightly kinder) Grandmother spoke sometimes about her love of offal, which disgusted him. Wobbly things; glands; greasy things. Hearts with the ends of tubes still visible; things you weed through. Stuff that boiled and fried and fugged up your kitchen with animal stench. Was it all chopped up, or milked and pureed and added to the Thai tapas?

They tried squid.

Little prawn toasts.

Costing six pounds and more; very expensive for a tiny thing no bigger than the smallest paper bag of pocket money sweet you could imbibe for seventy pence. He felt he had to eat. The squid: texture of shoe. The prawn toast: where it hadn't crackled in the frying, there was bread mush, looking like his baby sister's fat toe skins after bathtime. He wanted to cry out.

Now he remembered. *Sometimes I am afraid to close my eyes at night for fear of falling. I shall fall and fall and not get up and it must be like dying or not dying and everyone thinking you had but you could not say. If I swallow, I can die. And I will fall. I've seen the pipes and the tubes of a human body and they are not well organised and there was an advert on telly where a man recovered from serious illness and I saw it and thought, 'Great they can cure cancer,' and then the man went to a barbecue and choked because nobody knew what to do, which shows it could happen to anyone, however brave or clever or however well they had defeated a big illness.* But he must not show his mother. *And what if all this got back to Grandmother? She would be disappointed and trace it back to the wooden board when she had swept in, Maître Fromager, and she would make me tell her I did not like the Manchego cheese.* And on and on. And when the Pad Thai came, again in tapas portions, he ate a mouthful and went rigid, aghast also at the thought he might expectorate six-pound-eighty's-worth of noodles. Time was money and money was time, his dad said.

I need to go home.

Why?

I am going to choke.

You'll be fine.

What if I die?

Of course you won't die.

Why not? People definitely die of choking or it wouldn't be on the telly.

Well…

So you can't say it never happens.

And what is in here? In the Spanish–Thai muddle? All the things they might have mixed in or used to flavour it. Spanish omelette and heart and that nasty cheese that's like beasts in heat and melting straw and rotting things *and you said there were anchovies in it and things that tasted of lemon, but you didn't say they were lemon. I can't trust any of it.*

And the boy ran.

Mother caught him, as mothers do. Paid the bill. Over forty pounds for tiny things and indistinguishables and babies' bath toes and bits of organ and weird cheese. And the memory of his grandmother looking disappointed in that way she had. He wasn't like her friend's grandson who would try anything and like it, too. *Dear, dear. Boys today* and *I blame the mothers and if she had been my daughter I would have taught her how to raise a braver son.*

And on and on. Crying into the storm all the journey home. Frightened to sleep for fear of falling into a death crevasse, all littered with Manchego and nasty odiferous hauntings, which opened beneath his feet with each falling-to-sleep jump. Rigid then until overcome, at four a.m. and too tired, too immutable with fright to go to school the next day.

Keep it quiet. Keep the house battened down. It's hard to explain, this multi-layered suffering. If you took a food metaphor to deconstruct it – and you may know that planked or slated deconstructed food is all the rage just now – you could envision it like a trifle. On the bottom, there's the sponge and that's feeling guilty about being born and being a burden to your mother; the sherry soaked into the sponge is the shame drenched on you by (worst) Grandmother because you're not brave, not a trier, not pleasing or (alongside it) masculine enough like other grandsons. Then you've fruit. The fruit, first of all, depends on your poshness. Posh folk add kiwi fruit; the chavs, tinned strawberries; no matter, though, for the metaphor works either way: the pieces of fruit are the odds and ends of bad dreams and chunks of scorn and the lumber of certain failures, past and to come. The custard: it's viscous, like aortic blood or the gloop they drain out from the corpses before they flush; it's death, being trapped. Ah, the cream, now what is that? It's claustrophobia. You're in a classroom, with the popular kids, and they're pelting you on the back of your neck with the contents of their pencil cases and you don't turn around. You're told this won't last forever, but you're not sure because you were also reassured that choking wouldn't happen and it did to that man on the telly and you know your mum was bullied in school and she still hates the school run with your primary age brother because of the cool girls she isn't. So, the cream. Gloop. Look, a swamp. It's going to get you. Or is it quicksand, or the worst sort of snow, or pus and infection and it's seeping into you and you're fragmenting into shards but no one knows. And there, in bed at night, or in the classroom being pelted on the back of the neck with fine liners and protractors and somebody's horrid tooth-marked mouthguard, that's all there is.

Trifle kills. So do Thai tapas. And Grandma, affineur, with her hateful tidbits. And when you fall to sleep, there's the crevasse.

The boy sat rigid all night, for two nights: didn't go to school. The doctor was called, but the boy wasn't an emergency just yet. He gagged on egg and full fat carbonated drinks and little tiny morsels to stimulate his appetite and even milky things that Mother was taught to get into him, somehow. And on the third day, overcome by the tiredness, he slept and slept all day and half the night and when at last he woke he sipped with a straw and would never thereafter eat anything. But he drank and gagged, but drank because he had to. No good toast, or pizza or roast or pasta things. Just fluid, with his straw, under control and bland, so no beasts on heat, and that was that. From then on. Until he was almost a man, fully grown but still green and under-developed through attrition, being pumped and drained, too late to chew or bite; all gone.

At the wake, the glacé cherries winked from the top of the trifle, adorning the cream, custard, fruit and sherry-soaked sponge; a late addition for festivity's sake. It wasn't a kind wink.

seaside rock and other homicides

On the harbour of this fishtailed little town, there is a rock shop. No, not stones; we are not in Lyme Regis waiting for Mary Anning, Captain Curie and Miss Philpot. Not pretty rose quartz, or the feathers of a pressed crinoid. Ha, no. *Refined sugar*; for it's all they care for here. These people are not cultured, at least not in the way you understand. And I say a rock shop, but there's also floss in baby blue and flamingo, fudge as dense and acrid on your tonsils as wet cement (which you do not eat, but there are those who like to lick at quicklime and cornstarch so, ach, ach: don't judge).

And it's a special sort of rock shop, because you know how rock has letters, stretched to be sure, elastic all through it, spelling Rhyl or Great Yarmouth or Blackpool?

Well now, sometimes the letters in this rock have been used to spell other words.

Myfanwy Llewhellin runs this shop, and she used to be a sweet old girl. We used to call her Muffled Myfanwy, and she was as delicate and suffering as a pietà until she got her voice back and was corrupted, it is said, by an English erotic. She tends the till and shelves; the baskets of pretty fake pebbles and the floss; occasionally little treacle toffees which say, 'Thank you for feeding the cat,' and occasional biscuits made by Myfanwy's still mute, (still suffering) big-toed sister Anwen. And it's because Myfanwy's been corrupted by an English erotic and become more perfumed, upright and knowing, eyes like a sleepy cat's, that – or so it's said – she's been dabbling in the rock and making a few decisions that some might question.

Now, the reason Myfanwy was once muffled: suffering, as I said. Her vile husband and truculent son. One off with his whore and the other with her life savings, and she kind all her life but sometimes, break our hearts, our kindness is not repaid, is it. Or is it? I was saying.

When we meet love that sees us as what we are, we blossom. And that little flower, a blazon; some heat from a heart we thought we thought desiccant, and a loin we knew to be silent. Our imagination cannot, we think, be beguiled. All those things go with the love, and so, when the English erotic set eyes on Myfanwy and saw her shuffling in her little rock shop on the harbour, he thought not that her muffling was dull, but that it was mysterious. And when he saw her downy lip, a lumpen gait and a slight moistness of the nose, he saw not the fleshly inadequacies which we suffer, but something that was honest and devoid of vanity.

26

He saw the suffering all right and thought that it was borne with dignity and was pretty amongst the flamingo fluff and rainbow piles of sticks of rock. And Myfanwy saw that he looked at her and so her heart fluttered into the past and what she once was and back into the present now on the fishtailed harbour. And I suppose the Englishman did the same, because he was lonely and lacked glamour in the flesh too. But their eyes lit like those of hungry tigers because complicity – like bed, or the stars, or the best meal you ever had – may occur in a place you had thought desolate.

The English erotic did not, in the end, go home.

And the rock. Well now, sometimes they're at it late at night because they brought up machinery and began to make it on the premises and, oh, Myfanwy has worked like a dog. And then sometimes came the words in the rock and the decisions which some people in this sea town have come to question. Ah yes; they appear in the rock. It says the name of this sea town, this place, but there will be a phrase; a dare, like:

Oh, did you ever, and if not, why?

Or,

Will you tell me a secret?

Or

Which bad thing did you always want to do?

Myfanwy and her Englishman say nothing about this but, I tell you, the complicity is rampant, *rampant* in that little rock shop. And there's people who worry about the English erotic who's teased dear, suffering Myfanwy into life; these days she's quite talkative and sings too. And there's some that say that, late at night and early hours, there are muffled cries that might be coming from her still-suffering sister Anwen, and that Myfanwy is making her work the machinery because it's said that they're exporting. And what say the messages then?

Well now, I don't know what to think. Some days there's an odd feeling in our little fishtailed harbour town. And it's not like there's murder been committed, but there's strange folk coming into the shop and eyeing the two of them like they're all old friends and I, for one, am less inclined to go into that place these days. I'd advise you that, if you did, you should stick to the fudge, for there are no reports, as yet, of any text within.

a tale of tripe

Waking in the violet early morning, bathed in sweat and troubled by a night both eerie and vivid, Catherine searched her thoughts: 'What must I have been dreaming about?' It didn't take long, of course: *it was the tripe* – that and the matriarchs who washed it, handled it with such vigour and presented it with an expectant, nasty gleam in their eyes. Such sweet, creative fiends: mother and grandmother. In Mother's case, just dressing the tripe would have exhausted her for the day, sent her desperate to the fainting couch. In Grandmother's case, such dressing was simply a prompt to her killing another cow with the large-knuckled hands that terrified her grandchild so much.

Catherine winced: 'Grandmother and her man hands and downy arms – all wicked with a rolling pin and guarding the old stove with a vicious possessiveness,' thus the nasty crone would cry, 'Let no man come near my domain: I will slaughter them – smother them under the blanket of the beautiful tripe.'

That was it. That was the most disquieting image in the nightmare: Grandmother like Moloch waiting for a sacrifice over the fire; Mother's eyes dancing approval.

'Yes yes yes! Feed it to her! Now, now, *now!*'

'I'm so ashamed. I want a normal family and not to feel like this – waking, tripe-terrified.' So Catherine, voicing her deepest, wished aloud.

Mother and Grandmother were dead, but they found that no excuse. So, they visited Catherine regularly, sleeves rolled up, ready to cook. To rid herself of the present dreamscape, there was nothing for it: she must go downstairs and find a better image. Tea in a favourite mug was a good start, but Catherine found that her thoughts were leaping from vivid hue to hue – the reddest of pickled cabbage – to a turquoise preserving jar in which might have been preserved the innards of an unwanted relative. In Grandmother's pantry there was a hecatomb of conserves; the fruits of the season, incongruously presented in a chamber of horrors. There were pots of umber sludge; pickled eggs like eyeballs, bobbing in heavily sedimented jars; damp flagstones underfoot; a smell of sour, crawling mould. There were aprons hanging up, the prettiness of their floral decoration gone to hell in this place of condiments, good housekeeping and no hope. This was a room revisited on other troubled nights for Catherine; she could not let its scents and shapes leave her head, and the argot of this poky grey room whispered, 'Grandmother *knows*, just as *we all know*, and she and Mother will come for you.'

Here was a place of extinction, of annihilation, the meaning of such things terrifying in a dream but, even awake, the meaning is still only faintly, inchoately understood. 'This must be the worst combination: to know that someone is coming for you, but not to understand why, when or how. Or really what that has to do with pickles. Or tripe!'

Ah, the tripe – huge winding sheets of it. It smelled like death. When Catherine's nights were not punctuated by morbid pickles, siren-calling her to embrace their victim in death, she had nightmares of being cosseted in its velvet crushing embrace. The silky surface was puckered and hollowed. Somewhere else and in some other time, it might have been pretty; like a creamy-white mosaic you would want to touch. But in the nights, and when Grandmother or Mother served it up so triumphantly as punishment, the tripe blinked at her and writhed in its nasty pool of white sauce, encircled by effulgent lumps of onion. On its surface – its face, or was it its back? – were sucker pads like those on the arms of an octopus or some kind of strange sea plant that would caress and then swallow you whole, whispering of a lifetime of sin to you – just to compound the unpleasantness of this particular way to go.

Matriarchs hovering, the tripe came billowing clouds of vapour; it was cooked in a milky broth, all one at first, before you realised the unpleasantness of the discrete parts and sucky stomach-feet turned your (own) stomach. Between the two women, the silent challenge between mother and grandmother, it was a point of honour to make sure that the flour was never properly cooked off; thus, it lurked congealed in tiny mounds – but you didn't see it in the unmapped viscosity of the sauce. Didn't see the horrid little tumescence until you began to ingest it. Powder scattered in your mouth when the lump dissected. In a way, this was the worst horror:

'And the dust in my mouth as I sat between Scylla and Charybdis. Oh, a fine supper.'

Catherine had always blamed herself for the meals – for *why* they fed her so. For the spiteful sheets of tripe, served up like victory in chintz.

'My childhood looked so tidy from the outside; Mother and Grandmother were pillars of the community: first for cake in the village show; outstanding for a lemon curd; doyennes of the church flower rota. They prayed hard at the altar, shark eyes squeezed shut. I always thought it was me – it *had* to be me.'

'Send her out to the pantry, in the semi-darkness. Those eggs will frighten her a treat, make her more obedient. The mould on her hands! Ha!'

'Mother! Ah, that's the way to do it,' shrieked Grandmother, triumphant.

'But, say these homes must have been full of spite, hurt and venom to make Mother and Grandmother cook like that? Say it was *them* and I didn't deserve the tripe? Say it was wrong to shut me in there when I gagged on the tripe and onions and spat out the floury lumps without meaning to and they put me in the pantry like Jane Eyre in the Red Room?'

Catherine was not usually so bold. What was happening now that was making her behave differently?

Something was coming from the bookshelf. A small, dry, but nonetheless beguiling voice: 'Come here and open me up, Catherine.'

Now, Catherine was used to having a litter of imaginary friends. When your strange landlocked, ill-natured family surrounds you; when your nearest and dearest seem to close in on you with, *Bad, bad, bad and everyone knows about you*, then don't you *need* to tell someone? You can't tell real people because no one else seems to have a family as peculiar as yours.

'And how would I ever explain cooking as a way of throttling or suffocating an unwanted child?'

In the bad dreams, Catherine tended to see her relatives, Mother and Grandmother predominant, amassed, like the preserves, in a hecatomb. When at home, they tumbled out curses at her; out in the cold world, which welcomed their jam-making, their manners and determined smiles, they aligned in neat rows, pretty as pie. Who would believe Catherine about Mother and Grandmother? And how would she explain the chamber of soused horrors or the tripe? But here came a friend now; you might know her. To Catherine, she was ED; to the outside world, Elizabeth David.

ED wasn't the warmest sort, but her books smelled of spice and sunshine; of lemons and emerald parsley. Catherine took *French Provincial Cooking* from her shelf; it was from this that ED had been speaking to her. Catherine adored ED and all her books; could tell you about the 'pale rose pinks of the langoustines' which their author enjoyed with a fresh and sparkling appetite, alongside a bottle of Muscadet by the Seine. ED relished good butter, radishes with their leaves left on as God had made them; she saw the poetry and potency of a flat plate of Arles sausage and black olives.

'And the colour, ED; look at the colour of the things you ate and knew how to make! See the lovely creams and greys of shrimp; sunset-glow carrots. For you, even the dark things – the winkles and the cork stuck with pins; things that were muted or pebbly – those things became beautiful. *Beautiful* – flanking the colour, like a gentle relief. I want to eat like that, and I'd like to live like that. Embracing the darkness, yet knowing of its loving, numinous companion.'

ED, not one for a hug, and not particularly fond of metaphor, said, 'Well, do you have a sharp knife, a hot grill and a will of your own? I'm assuming you have a mandoline, some good bowls – and I will *not* share my kitchen with a garlic press. I must be firm about that.'

'Of course not; I know your feelings on garlic presses. I'm not sure I have a mandoline. I *do* have plenty of bowls, but some of them are chipped.' Catherine began to cry.

ED prodded her firmly in the back, coughed demonstratively and said, 'Chipped is fine, as long as we have at least a few white-lined brown dishes.'

'Why do we need these dishes – why must they be as you describe?'

Silence. A sigh. Then: '*Fresh contrast*. Now, it's time you stopped thinking about tripe. We are going shopping.'

'ED, I am dog tired.'

'That is no excuse. Not when we are going to compose hors d'oeuvres.'

Hurrying to dress, Catherine sighed disappointedly at her own drawn face and sad clothes, shuddered at the lingering dreams. Still, ED at least knew about the tripe, so they wouldn't be cooking *that*. They would grace a table with red tomatoes, yellow mayonnaise, sea salt and olive oil; a beautiful salad of grated carrot. And could it be celeriac that ED meant for the mandoline – all cut into the thinnest strips and highly seasoned with mustard, plenty of vinegar and a voluptuous, thick ointment of oil and egg?

Out they went, Catherine chatting silently to ED and now lighter of foot on their way to the wonderful market. But two shadowy figures watched her, curses dribbling from their lips with the last lappings of morning tea and vulgar gulps of toast with ochre marmalade. And inside Catherine's house, gently, timorously now, was a faint smell of the sea, a distant grating of nutmeg and a fresh twist of black pepper. '*Sacrilege.* I smell no wash day smell! I hear no slap of tripe against the pot!' said grey Grandmother and Mother.

Afloat, through thought and happiness, in Catherine's house now was the peaceful aroma of *potage bonne femme*: of cream, chervil, softly cooked potatoes and leeks, bathed in sweet butter. The shadowy figures cursed more, spitting unkind crumbs: '*Pain grillé aux anchois*? *Salade au chapon*? Get the little bitch. Boil up the tripe, Mother. *And bring out the ammunition from the pantry.*'

Catherine and ED, silently communing over their purchases, bought a mandoline and the requisite dishes, great bunches of green things for the *salade de saison*, dimpled lemons, celery, celeriac, lumpy tomatoes – things that promised succour. And life. But on returning to the house, dull wafts of tripe waited for her, as the shadowy figures took their joyful and vindictive hold of the kitchen. Garish red cabbage with a sweet, cloying smell sat with the cruel eggs on the worktop. *Amuse-bouches* of the sort you serve if you hate your guests; starters gussied up a little with hard bread, sea-foam milky tea and a cucumber cut into behemoth chunks. And the boiling tripe hissed milky sap.

'No matter,' said ED, walking briskly right through the shadowy figures, rolling up her sleeves and assembling a workstation next to the eyeball eggs. They leered as ED tasked Catherine with slicing the celeriac on the mandoline, while she concocted a highly seasoned dressing for its matchstick strips. Arles sausage was laid out on a large, flat, white plate, its fat coin slices overlapping; in the centre, a carefully built mound of black olives. Both glistened and invited. The tripe spat on, onions twisting and squirming round it, as ED and Catherine cut tomatoes and sprinkled them with gently snipped chervil – the dressing to be added '*absolutely*,' said ED, 'only when the diner wants to eat.' Catherine could feel on her pulse the metallic lure of a fine, misshapen tomato. They grated carrots almost, '*Almost*, I said!' to a purée, seasoning them carefully; made a wobbling heap of mayonnaise with fresh eggs, and olive oil from the first pressing. There was bread with a shiny, crackling crust, butter and some best quality anchovies.

'It is no shame to leave them in their tins if they are high-class brands,' barked ED. Catherine hurried to place back those she had already decanted.

The table of hors d'oeuvres, for a twelve o'clock lunch, was almost set. *Almost*. ED revealed a surprise. Out from a white plastic bag, secreted in the depths of ED's basket, came a single slithering sheet of tripe. 'For you.'

Tears pricked Catherine's eyes. 'No, not you too – please not you, Elizabeth. Don't make me cook it!'

From the room and the world all around came the laughter, the delighted grey shapes of Mother and Grandmother. 'Boil up the tripe, there's a good girl! *Choke choke choke* on the nuggets of flour!'

So ED was one with them, then.

'It had to be me, didn't it? I deserved what I got: a lock-up in the pantry; a stifling sheet of tripe and the unlovely curlicues of onions; gallons of white sauce and curses.'

The spectres grinned; the jarred eggs hummed, if ever a jarred egg could.

'Now *do be quiet*. Our lunch à deux first, then I shall teach you something new. You will have to boil the tripe briefly, but *then* you will grill it to a sizzling crispness, with a coating of egg and breadcrumbs, and serve it with a sauce tartare. A revelation, I think, it is called *tablier de sapeur* – or fireman's apron.'

'I can't.'

'You *will*.'

Lunch. The fierce, seductive rasp of the anchovy, crunch of good bread and the delicacy of finely cut celeriac. There were draughts of wine; ED passed knife and salad servers through the spectres of matriarchs. It was a celebration. Then lost sleep came and took her pupil.

On waking, ED had gone, but Catherine obligingly boiled the slice of tripe, cutting it with a certain passion into a neater rectangle. She basted it with egg, coated it with crumbs and grilled it until it was golden and the edges had caught on the flame. She ate the robust little apron with the sauce tartare that ED must have made for her, left with an uncommonly sweet note nearby:

'See off the spectres; try something new; *tablier de sapeur*: adieu; adieu.'

Hmmm. She almost liked the fireman's apron. 'It's not my favourite thing, but then neither is it the stuff of nightmares, thrust back to the sound of laughter into the dark pantry.

Ha! "Grill to a sizzling crispness," ED had said. A dynamic phrase; a confident one.'

Catherine threw wide the curtains, welcomed in the vestiges of the day and imagined scattering the grey tripe boilers and pickle hoarders into pieces. And she trilled, defiantly, 'Try something new. Mother, Grandmother, keep being dead now. Adieu; adieu!'

That night, Catherine dreamed only of the next chapters in her life: '*Soups* and *Eggs*, *cheese dishes and hot hors-d'oeuvre.*'

nanny lovett and pop todd

Did you ever hear tell of Nanny Lovett and Pop Todd, now deceased, with one pickled and the other soused? These two are sometimes still spoken about in these parts, *sotto voce*: they had an extraordinary pie shop, the fame of which spread all the way to the Greenwich meridian and back again, via Carmarthen and the new towns.

I am asking you because these two were my grandparents and, though naturally I am modest on the topic, I did learn something of the pie trade and am restlessly proud of what they did. They have led me to reconsider my future plans and reassess... certain risks and moral equivocations. I've been spending days basking in saporous memories.

Their house, with the pie shop attached, was on the quay, by the deep mud and the wrack; ah, it was lovely there, little boats coming in and the pot boys carousing. Like I said, people would come all the way from the Greenwich meridian to sniff my grandparents' baking and then take a pie home. Or a slice, because they were generous in size, their pies: bountiful and kind, although the contents had not been, in real and quick life.

So, Pop gave up his work as a barber when he met Nanny, who ran a not very profitable brothel on the docks. He would have given up everything for that woman because she could stop all the cars with her beauty. All ten of them by the harbour in Tenby, because we're going back a bit. And it wasn't only the beauty. *No*. There's a thing at work called *complicity*. It might involve crime and murder, but mostly a dark knowing and the sense that, within minutes of meeting the other, and from their first words, they are hot in your blood and your fate, just as the pastry of a good pie is sealed with a moist hand. That is that. I don't believe in love at first sight. I believe in complicity and its special heat. From that, and its immediate knowing, come love and a hot bed; a starry night in the quay and, in the case of my grandparents, a terrible, beautiful idea about pies.

There's a lot of cruelty in our world, isn't there? Where goggle-eyed dictators and influentials rule what is said. Where men are led by appetites of the wrong kind and lay their table not with bread and herbs but with lust and coldness. It's like a chess game of moving pieces to gain advantage, and what way is that to live? And you see, if you look closely, and if you get down there and smell the mud, titillate the sand on your tongue and suck at a blade of grass, well now you will taste the acidity that is born of cruelty. Here, in our beautiful country, the landscape, yellow beach and creek, would be free and sweet if not larded with these flavours. Ah. I startle you. You may not have known that country *had* a flavour because you hadn't been taught to flatten your face in the thrift or siphon gorse sugar. What have we done, we people that have blasted this world so?

But I will tell you another, more hopeful thing – and it is this.

There is a little time when, if you go out at dusk, whatever the weather, you can catch these bad thoughts and words of goggle-eyed dictators and influentials and of all men, before the land drinks them up and is spoiled. If you are sensitive – and you can be; my family could teach you, and there are many more than you can imagine who would do the same – you learn to see them and smell them before they land. Then you gather them in your hands and your calico bag, or they can be caught in a butterfly net, if you like. They don't look promising, like puffs of gauze or tiny cumulus clouds. But you take them to your kitchen, bags and nets of them, and as you go you feel they are getting heavier, beginning to solidify, and you cook them up with savoury herbs and spices, or sweet ones, follow your fetish, and they begin to disgorge a new and beautiful sauce – and that, my darlings, is when you put them in your pies, under a pastry crust which you have blessed and kissed. Know, then, that you will feed others well, and that you have kept dark things from saturating and embittering our landscape.

Well, what did you think was in the pies? Bramleys and blackberries? Veal and ham with a pretty little flag popped in the crust? That is nice, too, but I told you they were extraordinary pies. And did you think I meant murder pies, like in the old story? A demon barber and his neighbour, the appalling baker? Ah. Well, that did happen too. Because when Nanny and Pop couldn't catch all the bad thoughts and words, for there were so many, they did resort to other methods. Those reserved for the very worst sort of person. Like the corrupt judge who victimised the poor tenants on the farms down our way; the nasty bigamist man and the batterers, or those who were deeply in ego and hurting all around with things horrid and incorrigible. Ah yes. Well, that the content of these sorts of pies was discovered would explain why Pop was soused in the Swansea prison and Nanny in the Carmarthen asylum, after a fashion. And that was sad, especially because those pies full of sweet and toothsome numbles and haunches were thought to be *exquisite*.

So, I miss them, Nanny and Pop, and I miss their confections and that is why I will open my own pie shop soon, here on the quay, in our blazing summer. Come and visit. Come along with your calico bag and butterfly net and protect this landscape of ours. Bake with me? And for the rest. Those pies not stuffed full of richly sauced puffs of gauze and calico cloud? Ah, well now. I'd advise you not to disabuse me. Come, sit down, my darling. I believe in complicity and its special heat.

See what I have. Eat.

henry and his surfeit of lampreys

'… re-turning from lumting at St. Denys in the 'Wood of
Lions,' he partook of some lampreys, of which he was fond,
though they always disagreed with him ; and though his
physician recommended him to abstain, the king would not
submit to his salutary advice ; according to what is written : –
"Men strive 'gainst rules, and seek forbidden things.'"

Historia Anglorum, **Henry of Huntingdon, 1129 and 1135.**

Tell me: have you ever cradled a thrashing eel or formed a
crucible of elvers and made them slip here and there through
your fingers? Unguent, vicious and unknowing. Have you
ever met a lamprey face to face, where, in certain puddles, it
doffed its hat before throwing said ornament into the irises
and jumping into your mouth?

King Henry of England loved a dispute and a delicacy
and, as we learn from records of the twelfth century, he
particularly adored what was forbidden – delicious though
bad for him – and loved to thrash out arguments at dinner,
like a sort of coulis, had those been extant in the High

Middle Ages. He also loved copious mistresses, mead and, occasionally, a nun, though this is not the whole picture of a man; hot wrangling, sex and appetite never are. Though they are a clue, yes.

And there was another Henry, a more modern one, who shared some interests with this late king. He fell into arguments and liked them and had an abundance of appetite, which was not generous, but desperate; risky. He had dabbled in puffer fish, in *fugu*, and told the chef to take less care; he was a careless mycologist but had survived thus far and, with the most reprobate of his friends, was charmed by overindulgence in absinthe. He knew a man who planned to imbibe a live octopus and another who'd emerged alive after eating troughs of unripe akee, though he was often queasy and suffered from vertigo on stairs, the fool. The secret was knowing when to stop. And he did.

He *thought* he did.

Henry, unpleasant Henry, liked to bore and worry. And he appreciated the fact that lampreys do, too. They fiddle and slime and ingratiate their way into the body of a fish and suck the life, but the only people he knew who dabbled in them were local fishermen. Yet (he had done his research, like all good gourmands), these creatures were highly appreciated by the Ancient Romans. During the Middle Ages, they were widely eaten by the upper classes throughout Europe – particularly during Lent, when eating true meat was prohibited, on account of their meaty taste and texture. The apocryphal story of King Henry adds a garnish to this. He would fish and imbibe, solo. And catch our modern Henry did, in the Cleddau River, in mid-June, a sweltering day. Up they came, younger from the troughs they had dug and older with teeth, even on their tongues; some attached to pike and perch, which he admired then threw back, before pressing their slimy bodies with a *Well done, boys. Oh, that was a catch.* Henry shook with pleasure on the bank of the river; shook as he carried a haul back home, up to where he lived at the mouth of the Cleddau estuary, with a sad woman who called him her own and had no name.

And in the kitchen, he could not resist. He dispatched a few, admiring their peculiar and horrid heads, open like a toothed cavern, violent and red. Chopped and prepared for frying. But, just as he had sometimes sucked down elvers and longed to lick at the entrails of the *fugu*, Henry could not resist a bite of the slippery creature raw. He looked it in the mouth, bit down and bored into the lamprey as the lamprey-kind had done to pike and perch. And it was still. For a moment, before it jumped. Right down his gullet. He might have died, but no. A mercy. This lamprey found a warm home and dug in its teeth. There was a sound, from within his viscera, like a whistling, the sound of a dull cry across ice, and other lampreys jumped, siren-called by it. All animals have a song.

And that is almost the end of the story. They didn't kill him, though these days he is a dreadful thing – a papery husk – and there's less hot wrangling. No energy, see. And the woman with no name with whom he lived has gone with John the Bait. There are no more mistresses, just an endless need to procure and, occasionally, the dull cry as the lampreys die and call for more, so that Henry is compelled to fish in the Cleddau River and cannot prevent more of the creatures from jumping into his guts. He is forever hungry, forever feeding, with crumbs only for himself.

Ah, kings of the table.

Did you know that King John fined the City of Gloucester about £250,000 in our modern money for failing to deliver the annual gift of a lamprey pie to him at Christmas? That poor watery city has been stuck with delivering a royal pie every Christmas until 1836, and since then for coronations and jubilees. They even have to employ a special person, The Procurer of the Lamprey (he has a chain less resplendent than the mayor's), because the scarcity of lampreys in our British Isles has meant that these pies are made from specimens from North America. Oh, why don't they just go down the Cleddau River in Pembrokeshire, where the lampreys are big and loud and strong? Or dig into Henry's chitterlings for some fine exemplifications?

Still, poor Henry. There was one thing he didn't know about lampreys (and, in fact, I cannot help but wonder whether King Henry went the same way and that the reason for his choleric was that he had lampreys hanging on inside until his demise). You see, a man may enjoy a surfeit of anything. A surfeit of lampreys.

But, sometimes, lampreys like a surfeit of man.

hot cross buns, sharp teeth and a tongue

'I am cross,' said Old Ted, 'about the buns. It isn't fair. At my time of life and with everything that's happened to me and I feel like crying. I do, and it's not just the buns, is it?'

So Penelope, just someone who talked to cross Old Ted, started to have conversations in the street and on the bus with older folk about how they objected to the ubiquity of hot cross buns. It was the ubiquity, this survey of elderly folk revealed, which had spoiled them. Same with bread and the cheese, spoiled by the bounty of mass production, the same but worse, because the buns were special. They were annual. Then, it would have been like Christmas cake in July. But not now.

Penelope hadn't intended to spend so much time with the olds, who chattered like parakeets, but was drawn in.

Their teeth sometimes offended her sensibilities, but she cloaked herself in kindness and went on with the survey.

'I bet you get Christmas cake in July these days and I can't bear it,' said cross Old Ted on the bus, another day. 'Once, they appeared at Easter or you made them. You did not get them all year round and, though memory may not ratify here, apparently, they did not used to be so doughy and squashy. I talked to my neighbour about this on the bus last Thursday. He calls me "Boy" (not Ted, he's Bill), I'm eighty to his ninety-five. He was on his way to hospital; his wife died recently and he had just recovered from pneumonia. He was on his way to hospital because of the aneurism, though. They thought he was better now, but he was going for a follow-up. "One of these days I won't come home," he said. "I don't get out much either. Although I did go to Asda to get some hot cross buns and, well, I was so disappointed by how doughy and soft they were, not like—" And I said, "Bill, I could have told you that they were not going to be like... What were you thinking?" To which he retorted that I was to be more respectful because his wife had just died and an aneurysm wasn't funny either. And I was "Boy" to him.'

He licked his sharp little teeth, and Penelope observed that the work of the sandman had not yet been swept from a rheumy eye. But she thought, with the kindness cloak on, 'Well that's a dead wife, an aneurysm, a hospital visit, cross Old Ted on the bus and a whole lot of disappointment in the community about the buns.' She wasn't a natural cook but didn't entirely like sadness in old folks.

So she invited them all for tea, and herewith the invitation, thus: 'I hope you will come to my house for tea and feel a little more cheerful because we are going to have home-made hot cross buns. And overleaf is a hot cross bun recipe, just as my grandmother kept it. I've got her notes with it, too: "Soft but substantial, and you can also get the top crisp. Plenty of spice. Serve with tea." This is the recipe I've used and I've included it so you can make your own at home! I've given metric measurements as those are obviously the ones I use, but I can help you convert them if you would like.

For 14 hot cross buns

25g dried easy blend yeast

300ml warmed milk

A pinch of love!

Then 400g plain flour, sieved, with 25g of unsalted butter rubbed in and a pinch of salt

50g caster sugar

1 or 2 teaspoons of mixed spice

50g sultanas

To make the glaze and get the cross on top, keep to one side 2 tbsp of water and 2 tbsp of caster sugar

Add the yeast to the warmed – not hot – milk and then mix in the flour followed by everything else. Leave this to rise in a warm place for about twenty minutes, add a little more milk if it seems too floury and knead it just a little. Make the dough into fourteen balls and put them onto prepared trays. Cut a cross in the top of each one with a small very sharp knife, leave for another twenty minutes (they will grow!) and then cook in a hot oven until they are golden. It will take about twenty-five minutes, during which time you make a simple syrup for the glaze by dissolving the sugar in the water. While your buns are still hot, apply the glaze to the cross. Eat while they are still hot or toast later. They will be a triumph! And if you want some extra spice, dust them lightly with cinnamon or nutmeg before you serve and maybe even sprinkle with golden caster sugar. But just a little. Best served with butter in the middle, salted or unsalted.

'I expect you all enjoyed that! Feel free to share it with anyone else!

'Come at 3 p.m. this Thursday. No need to RSVP.'

And on Thursday, she was sure of a full house. Penelope waited and waited. Three-thirty. Four. Four-fifteen. No. *Where were they?* She'd made the buns; was so proud. Now, they were wrinkling, and everything was spoiled. At seven a note was pushed through the door. It was from cross Old Ted from the bus: 'It was nice of you to invite us, and I feel bad we didn't turn up. But there's drinking and whoring on Thursday afternoons, and then you did say not to RSVP. But for future reference: fuck off and don't patronise your elders, there's a good girl.'

Penelope shoved the wasted buns in the bin.

Old people were, after all, so horrid. And instinct should have informed her about the sharp teeth.

shame

I loved Nutella chocolate spread. I loved it straight out of the jar on finger and even on thumb. Sometimes, I had been known to dip a finger in the syrup, too. But only a finger, as I do have limits. My ex-husband hated this; said I was grubby. Told his mother. I was a lard-arse, too. Said I was covered in oily accretions and his mother said, 'Oh she'll attract the dust, that one.'

And I loved the sunset dust in the bottom of the tortilla chip bag. He hated that, too. Tortilla chips in front of the telly and there's me waiting to hoover up the leftover particles, bag on face, dredging the cream sofa as I went.

So too I loved the Parmesan rind. He introduced me to parmesan. Before my days with him, the only cheeses I'd ever had were those squashy triangles, Wotsits and whatever the cheapest Cheddar was. That was because I was common. And attracted dust. He took me to a dairy and made me understand cheese. He said, 'Look, this is washed rind,' and, 'This is proper, unpasteurised cheddar, not what you're used to,' and it was an education, but then I cried in the car after my lesson. The next day he took me to a cheese shop in town and explained that there was that sneeze-powder, pretend parmesan, and there was the real thing, properly aged. And, though I cried again, I did learn a thing or two and, eventually, I stopped crying and grew an idea or two. These days, when I've used up all the parmesan, I keep the rind to add savour to soups. I then take the rind, gloriously chewy from simmering away, and wolf it. This could be done in a dark kitchen. I like to do it in a dark kitchen because, when I started growing ideas – which he, ironically, helped me seed, plant and nourish – I started to realise that shame can be *delicious*.

Here's something else that I loved and don't think is really anything to be ashamed of. Other people have been shocked by my habit of chiselling off all the stuck-on bits from, say, the roast potato dish. His mother said this made me look feral. So did he. But all the time I was becoming more deft with chisel and knife. I did the same thing with a shepherd's pie or cauliflower cheese dish, chipping away with spoon and finger, wiping my fingers on my skirt. No apron, little homemaker.

He called me a lard-arse and I thought, *I am, I am*, but there was a larger thought which said, *It's not right; to call you that*. And, *You should eat him up*.

I discovered the ersatz and the things he thought inferior; I ate a ring of prawns from Iceland not long ago. And then there were other things: a whole big bag of liquorice comfits scarfed down in the car. Or that rather expensive all-natural Australian liquorice marketed as low fat, but calorically ruinous. Crackling. Cold and preferably around midnight, when slightly pissed. He never drank much because he savoured it, of course; I managed to make excuses to avoid his wine club. I just drank. That made more things bearable. And I began to grow more ideas. What could I do to disgust him more?

As often as I could, I'd be making fairy cakes for the children and leaving rather a lot in the bowl for licking out. By me, not them. I sucked a mango stone in bed. Once even brought to bed a cornet of winkles, accompanied by a corn stuck with pins, for winkling, on our seaside holiday. I ate pie in the bath; got chickens and killed an old, defunct layer in front of him, for the pot. POP. You pull their necks, if you don't get them over a broom handle. He went green. Good. I made a filigree of strange things in aspic for his gourmet friends: diver-caught scallops; tinned mandarin oranges; and said, 'Here: some evaporated milk as sauce,' and it was trimmed up in a Denby jug. He started coming home later and later.

Good. The first night I thought he just wasn't watching the time; the second, I knew it was avoidance – of me, my aberrations. I sat on the sofa, in my tiger onesie, and ate cold baked beans from the can, dipping in carrots. Because I liked it; in case he came in and I could confirm the revulsion. At Christmas, I got up in the middle of the night, noisily as I could, and sucked down the satsuma from the toe of my Christmas stocking, crunched sugared almonds and put a chocolate Santa in the bed, next to my hot water bottle, to percolate across the Egyptian cotton he insisted on.

And he called me a lard-arse. Said, *You're no stranger to the sweet trolley and you're common and disgusting and I don't know what I'm doing here.*

By New Year he was leaving me; he already had someone else, all amuse-bouches and tidy hair. A sexy nightie and a soft, brushed dressing gown. Ugh. He started tidying up his things, with little MINE stickers; I did the same, on pot noodles and tinned corned beef; a Fray Bentos steak and kidney you can eat on your own, without peas or greens, even if you're not camping. He was ready to go. And the funny thing was this: did I mention my knife skills? I learned butchery from my grandfather, so they were good, really good, my knifings. I thought about it; about carving him up and putting him in a pie and then I thought, *no*.

Let neat, sweet Morsel-Delores in accounts have him. He's a bitter cud; he's gristle. He's sour, but not in the good green mango amchoor kind of way (I'd learned about spices), so you have him, love.

And I? Well if a story's all about the ending, then I put on my tiger onesie and sat and waited. Sat with bowls of olives and shreds of spam and pickled eggs and little things that didn't go. And I had a watermelon for colour, cut up like a beautiful jewel, and instead of dyspepsia, I got joy. Quiet man, messy, happy; *he* came round. We sat there, on the Doritos dust sofa. In years to come, we crunched in bed and ran and played because much depends on dinner, but also on your company. Don't you think? I really am a lard-arse these days.

But.

My skin glows with the love and oh, the things that go flying and I don't know if I am a lard-arse because I don't look and he says to me, 'You're beautiful and I love you,' and we put on our tiger onesies together and it is forever. Plus Twiglets and dippy Hellman's. But then, if he tries it on, I've the chisel and the knife, oh my oh my, or I'll choke him with a nutmeg. Or two.

cucumber sandwiches

Cucumber sandwiches. High tea somewhere in the past, which is another country. Cucumber sandwiches are those that you often neglect to prepare. Too predictable. Too homey. Maybe so predictable that you forgot all about them and how extravagantly delicious they were. But let me tell you this: never trust a sandwich. It can be a thing of snide rebuke; its constituent parts laugh at you and rasp your throat. If you go to a tea party, don't say I didn't warn you.

But on this particular afternoon, the sandwiches had not been forgotten, and that was because there was murder in the air. Quiet, pretty murder; a press of palm and a *so nice to see you* and a hot-cold eye. A screened porch in Virginia and an English-style tea. Hot tea, iced tea, the cucumber sandwiches – without crusts, to be sure – ham sandwiches, strawberry shortcake and an English fruit cake. In Britain, the spread was similar, minus the iced tea, with those same sandwiches, but also country ham, scones with some home-made jam, and rock cakes made by a child of the family on a bored and stony Sunday afternoon.

In Virginia, it was stiflingly hot. The guests came, grateful for the swooping fans and the tea and the cool of those lovely cucumber sandwiches. It all looked *a picture.* But the hostess was simmering, although nothing was said. There was a sighing that was just about audible, but no one mentioned it or asked what was the matter. Someone might have wondered whether there were a fainting couch in the house, for this was suffering pure and simple: *I invited you but I do not particularly want you in my house. I wish I had never thought of it.* Back in Albion, the gloves were off. It didn't take long for a comment to be made. *Did you not like the scones? You clearly didn't want to come, did you? Why does no one else make an effort? It's always me.* At least it was quiet, there on the Blue Ridge – but the atmosphere would do well to be cut with a knife. As an experiment. In Britain, the crumb-covered knives had been slammed down on the worktop and the washing-up neglected, an index of how little she was appreciated. Left there. Let someone else see to it. *Or her.* No more cutting today, then.

Outside, summer blazed on. Inside, we resorted to near-fisticuffs or a glint of resentment in a smiling face. Depending on where we took our tea that day. And on some days, when a tea was called, not everyone found their way home.

shadow babies' supper

On a graceful, desolate street, in a cold house, there were three rocking chairs, where three tiny forms sat formally, just so and waiting.

The chairs had black frames, rush seats; they were immaculate; still. No one, she said, was to hurry at or hassle these chairs, and they sat silent with their lovely occupants: three still infants. At least that was what I thought when I first looked in the formal front room. It was a shock, as I walked in with a clutch of young, hot-blooded and real children of my own, lowering our voices as I'd trained them to do, in these parts, on Sundays especially. And, do you know, in the lap of each lovely occupant was a delicate biscuit and a shrivelling fruit, shaped by the desiccant air of the cold house.

Here was I. Getting used to motherhood. Travelling alone. No mother of my own, hungry for that kind of love, and carrying a childhood that was rearing its head and causing commotion as I came to terms with wrongs I could not right. All I could do was release suffering to the elements and love my own darlings.

A graceful, desolate street: I needed straightforward, not a chilling oxymoron, but there was no way out, because I'd said I'd come and had to be kind. To understand a new life of which I was now part. And in the graceful, desolate street, something hung in the air; I'd say it was a kind of hunger, that something was at the corner of your eye and whispering to your timid ear. It said that in this street and in this house and on these tiny chairs there waited ghastly spirits and creatures to nip at your heels and lap you up. Revenants and wights that were appetitive and governed by the desire of their tongue and by the pain in their dour hearts. Or did I, and did you, imagine such a thing?

Did you imagine it, or could you see little bites on the pretty biscuit and the desiccated fruit in each lap? And did you trace a crumb on a dainty lip or hear a mew of mastication at each little person?

Rocking chairs. Well now, everyone in the South has rocking chairs, don't they? Out on the porch, in the parlour; they're a staple. But in the miniaturised form, I found, they held a terror for me. I couldn't help it. The *rock, thump, rock, thump*, a classic horror trope – it was almost funny. But the notion of something small, sentient and evil (my imagination travelled fast) occupying it was appalling. I realised my chest was a compaction and that I was stammering *hello* and saying how *so very nice* the porch was, with its swing seat and dignified ferns. And all the while, wraiths licked their lips.

At the time, my two eldest were tiny, and this house I went into – we will say it was in Dalton, Georgia – I had thought, fantasised, once, that it could be a kind of home from home. I'd been raised with death all around me, gasping and screeching; sometimes laughing. But I was not afraid, because the pain of living with death had gifted me imagination and purpose. But as I entered this house, I felt a different thing. Something deathly, yes, but not something kind. Instead, a breath around me that said here was danger; a tomb – but a living one. Even now, I cannot quite explain all this, but I think it's a nexus of hostility and vengeance that smiles and makes tea and kills you slowly. Kills you with grace and good manners. There is nothing more terrifying than knowing you are unsafe because there is no love for you. *Oh no no no*. And then you scent the hunger; something small and ghastly in its appetite, though for what?

And don't you ever catch things at the corner of your eye? Things moving which shouldn't? A grimace from an inanimate object or a spark of light from a cold dark thing? That, too.

I had to go into this house, though I felt its wrongness as the screen door opened.

'Welcome,' she said to me. Then, to the two small children, 'I know you won't touch anything unless I give you permission. And then, when the children have played, we will *eat*.' Her eyes flamed and her gaze slid to the three rocking chairs with their settled occupants. She was the Keeper of the House.

And do you know, that in the rush and timetable of your daily life, you're on a veneer. In my experience, I've found that a dull horror has broken in, now and then. Where a smiling face cracked its plaster behind closed doors; where a pretty house gave way to a mausoleum because the living had been so disappointing. That's what happened here, and yet... knowing all this, understanding its logic, I was still afraid, and remain so, of the impact of the Keeper of the House and of the occupants of those rockers. 'We will eat,' she had said. And the *we* was the beastly dolls, too. They would be at table, drinking it up. Drinking up the adoration of the Keeper of the House, but also their inky eyes would enquire how they would slurp you up; what they would take. I knew it. But who was mad here?

I was afraid of peculiar, insane things. Being eaten, bitten, lapped up; thinking that if enough quiet madness were to seep in, my pretty children would turn doll and cannibalise, freed from all true civility like King Duncan's fine horses the night of his regicide, when it was said, by the old man, that they did eat each other.

How should all these thoughts crowd in, of appetite and famished things? In my head, I said the Welsh word for longing: *hiraeth, hiraeth, hiraeth.* And said it again and again, to replace the crowding bad things.

Ah. Horror. *Alarum.* 'Where there is no imagination, there is no horror.' Not so.

The still infants had ivory skin, long, real hair, a flush on their cheeks and sawtooth eyelashes. They wore Sunday best, little aprons, and one had white gloves, like a proper altar child. Or, I thought, like a cold-blooded murderer-babe who'd trot an innocent before her and sacrifice it, say a little prayer and tweak the florals in the aisle, like a good, good girl. Sit back down, hands in lap. In the alabaster jaw, shot-gold tiny teeth, ready to nibble. Come slithering across the floor; bite at you, draw blood and love it.

'Ugh,' said the boy. The real boy. 'Those dolls are creepy. I hate them.'

'Shhh,' I said. 'They are special, and you mustn't go nearer.' But I hated them too.

The three infants in the rocking chairs looked on. I looked at them. What if I were to shake them – what would happen then? Why would a grown woman even think this? Well, I know. Their solid eyelids would slap back and forth, their real hair would be coarse tendrils over my arms and the pins in their Sunday best would scratch and scrape.

Oh, the hair. My imagination ran wild. There was a family not far away, gravestones in the front garden, touched by the Spanish moss from the live oaks. It was a ramshackle old place; every Southern cliché an outsider could hurl at it. They said, the Best Ladies of the town, that the old mother there had sold her hair before she went under the red earth, to pay for her coffin, because impoverished. I remembered that now; half shudder, half laugh, remembering, too, Faulkner's Cash holding up the box he was working on so his dying mother, Addie Bundren, could see it and approve it, as she lay dying. In this town, with the house and the rocking chairs for the bloodless infants, people whispered, and that's how I heard the story about the hair selling.

A silent tea. Dry and polite sandwiches; all about will, not appetite, elbows in, table conversation. In the silence of a heart, I was still thinking about selling your hair, gargantuan plaits, and assessing your coffin, while making table conversation, with the children kicking each other and trying not to show the pain. Then night-time, when in Georgia the wind swoops in across the screened porch before the storm. It's like a scream. At home (I so wanted that now), the cree of the curlew would be looming loud against the upping air and the movement, the shivering all around, but it was good. The place meant you well. I once found the face of a doll amongst the sea glass and the cowries and I hurled it back into the sea. The kelp and wrack battened down on it, while the spume breathed, 'Gone.' And at home, there were no arid sandwiches, but only a generous table; at home, hunger was for rightful things: to eat up the sorrow of others with a song; to drink in a purple headland with your eyes and be full. Oh.

Now, with the creatures nearby and their Keeper wishing harm to us but never, ever expressing so – it's not done; it isn't mannerly, speaking so plainly of bad emotions – my instinct was to take my two small children and pelt out into the Georgia night. But where? And I wasn't sure it was an emergency, so how could I run to the kindness of strangers?

But I sensed my children felt disgust and annoyance, not fear; they were a comfort to me.

Now, across a dark sky with its flashes of cruel light, the storm took up more, doors rattled and the Keeper of the House – mother, I supposed, of the bloodless infants; feeder – put the patchwork comforters around them, and against the rattles: 'I don't care for draughts.' But the fire was not lit. Why? Perhaps because you wouldn't want to bother the delicate skin of the dolls, old as time, with hair aeons old, from the old lady who'd breathed her last not far away in The Hollows. She'd rolled over and died in her saggy bed near-bald, because she'd sold her hair to pay for a box and so that some pretty little people could be crowned up right.

And a careful little girl, as the Keeper of the House was then, could cradle them and sing and spit if another came near. 'The dolls are looking at me,' said the younger boy.

'Don't be stupid,' said the older one. 'But they are weird.'

I looked then, properly. Saw that their clothes were perfect, little hands in laps; a frill here and there, at the collar, gussied up so it undulated just right under their chins. And when I looked again, I saw they were part of a tableau, for between their chairs, as if the dolls were to get down and play, were hairless teddy bears, a russet wooden train and then, for reasons I could not understand, an antique croquet mallet, no hoops or balls. Why? So, they could attack us, then sit back down; they were bloodless, so who could suspect? Or just to show how beautiful it all was. Should be? Childhood, when expressed properly, prettily and silently? Bloodlessly. At the corner of my eye, a flash of sharp tooth and a tear; a spot of slaver on lace collars.

We talked sotto voce and unnaturally about school and manners; vitamins, right behaviour, walks and reading; church and how life is better for good little boys who know right from wrong; and then went gratefully to lie in the high old beds. But here was no close and holy darkness, for the youngest could not resist: back he went to the rocking chairs, took the croquet mallet and hit each infant, cracked it soundly on each nasty little head. I ran, fearing terrible things. He'd not hit them hard, but to a small child, it was natural inclination and, also, revenge on the horrid little creatures. Silence.

Back to bed, children. But no. She had been instantly alert.

The wailing started and we ran towards it: 'He hit my dolls! He hit them! Oh oh oh!' Stammering sorry, all fled to the high beds and the boys drifted off, not proud exactly but, I sensed, vindicated. Children have a natural sense of justice and that some hauntings are good, some bad. And, as I said, I was more scared than they were. I'm a little ashamed to admit that. It seemed to me the dolls had more slaver on their pretty lace collars. Like dog drool; nasty and appetitive.

I stayed awake for hours, listening to the muffled doors and the quavering: '*Oh oh oh. Momma's here now. It's okay. The boy was nasty, wasn't he? Shhh. Shhh. My sweet babies. It's okay now. Momma's here. Momma feed you, pretty babies. My babies. Oh oh oh.*'

I've seen many things. Been touched by them, even. Felt an insubstantial hand on my shoulder, a whisper of old times, fancied I saw a ripple in the earth when I prayed at fresh graves; at twilight, above the sea, I go alone to visit my Dead Dears and croon to them of paths on the headland, memories in sea caves and the plight of the blackberry harvest this year. I feel them around me, in the half-light, and their presence is good and there's that beautiful susurration, 'Do not be afraid!—' 'Noli Timere' from the schooled ones and a bit of 'Paid ag ofni' from the proper Welsh. That's a good haunting and it's my family. But those bloodless infants, out there across the Atlantic, they care nothing for the living and, I swear, if they could speak, they would tell you that they seek only the protection of the Keeper of the House and to sit, for eternity, undefiled in their Sunday best. And they do not care who is unloved or damned to Hell along the way. And time enough, and without the hit of a wise child, could it be that they would come at you, lickety-split? Split a vein with a bite; scoop out your soul and freeze it for sorbet and to laugh at how weak you were.

Well, bless the child with his rueful mallet who hated them and censured their horrid porcelain heads and trafficked hair.

I have to go back to this house. Someday soon. The two small boys are big now, but they remember it; the very oddness: the silence of the house. But now I have another one, too: a small child. And I've noticed that the Keeper of the House has, in the prettiest of formal letters, expressed more interest in the littlest one; he is rumoured to be the ps and qs and malleable boy. In bad dreams, I see her tugging at his arm, crooning: 'Come sit. Won't you come to me?' Like I said, I have to go back and have to be sympathetic, but he's not leaving my side for a whispered conversation or to play by the doll tableau. I don't know what fear might take hold or could be murmured. What might be imbibed: spirit or very blood. And none of us knows how hard a bloodless infant can kick when it's strong from getting all the love.

the choracle

Donna Griffiths was unlucky in love. All these children by cad after cad, and the children were fine, if testy and occasionally busy on remand and correction, but the cads were not ever fine and left.

'Oh, this time. He'll be the one. I *know* it. It will work out.' But no. And she deserved better because, since cradle days, she'd never been properly loved. It had always been conditional, provisional or, with her mother, second to other folks' daughters or, with the cads, second to the pub and harbour whores or their nasty Alsatian hound *who was a sweet boy* WOULD YOU LOOK AT HIM. NO ONE LOVES YOU LIKE THEIR DOG DO THEY BOY? And she'd properly tried, dusting off the cads and getting the kids through school while the neat-and-tidies eyed her, as middle-class mothers do; the way they sometimes eye the person less fortunate than themselves for whom they would feel compassion, yet slough it off because *that kind of mother*. Well, *she* can't be clever or good; she might have wit but could never have genius, and more to the point, associating with her, standing too close, brings bad luck. You'll get linked with her and the dilapidation will spread osmotically into you.

This is something that all mothers know but few speak of. Luck of this sort is never structural but stitched up with pub nights and sluttish pickled eggs slapped in salt and vinegar bags. That kind of luck. *That kind of woman*. Mother. The jarred pickled egg to your smashed avocado on sourdough.

Now, Donna the pickled egg had turned fifty. She looked thirty-eight, but either is the age when women are expected, by some, to turn invisible, and they ingest that and buy a new frock and worry about their upper arms and whether they wobble or that they should stop eating, invest in needle procedures, peels, unguents or a blind older man for bed. That is all wrong, as we shall see.

It all started when Donna Griffiths threw a party for her eight-year-old, the youngest of the tribe. The usual. And this child requested a chocolate fountain. 'Mammy. I'd love one. And we can dip strawberries in it. And bananas, bits of apples.'

She assented. 'Of course, my darling,' and went to buy, laden by the thought of expenses: the disco man, party bags, all the paraphernalia our young like to wallow in. Later, mixing the chocolate that accompanied the fountain, she was revolted, yet taken by the unusual waxy nature of the substance. It was unlike any chocolate she had ever met and seemed, to her, to flow against type and gravity; it was oily and viscous; full of life, like mercury making its pretty menisci and then flowing down.

'Yessss, a chocolate fountain!' hooted the troupe of children at the party, while the other mothers clucked outside: runs, circuits, fancy kitchen islands and prosecco. At first the children were in a line, neat and sensible, thus proffering the strawberries Donna had left in the nearby bowl. Then, stuffed with sugar and viscosity, well-oiled children misbehaved and plunged in other items; ersatz crudités: in went celery, Wotsits, cheese and onion crisps. Sediment began to erupt, like crude with grit in it. *No no no.* Donna switched off the chocolate fountain. She sat, waving them off, eyeing the trounced room.

Bubble and drip.

A hollow noise.

Bubble and drip.

'Mammy, look!'

Bigger bubbles, swirling, the fountain fizzing, becoming turbulent; a river of chocolate.

Up and up came the chocolate fountain, switch thrown by an unseen hand, or command, by an ethereal, slathered in cocoa butter. It could not be, yet it was. One of the smashed avocado mothers, a Mrs. Sylvie Roberts, came searching for a child's coat. 'Oh,' and, 'Oh my God,' for in the fountain came shapes; mocking like gargoyles, startling. Now the face of avocado on sourdough. 'Look, Mammy, it's making a picture of Mrs. Roberts,' and it was. 'And that looks like Mr. Roberts but not with her!'

Mrs. Roberts shrieked and called for the other smashed avocados.

'Oh my God. It's me. It's you!'

Vistas of what ifs and maybes and happenstance in the lives of others; feature wallpaper peeling in Mrs. Ellen Jones's houses; a cracked, glittery kitchen island no longer splendid in a rich and proper house. Every so often a pickled egg jumping up smiling, buoyant, an alabaster egg with the face of Donna Griffiths above a bag of salt and vinegar, sometimes brandishing some pork scratchings; not one for the posh crisp or the cornichon, stamping those into the swirling pub carpet.

'Oh my God. It's Donna Griffiths! She's got magic.'

The fame of the choracle and of Donna spread widely, at least into the church hall car park. All the women crowded around, faces caving, howling, but not running away from the choracle: Donna and the fountain. Seer and tablet. And the fountain bubbled like a geyser and threw shapes of the women and vistas and feelings into the room and they felt her sadness and knew that theirs was no less.

The next day was different. The smashed avocados eyed the pickled egg: they'd seen a new type of horizon, or maybe just within. Donna met a new cad that afternoon and the women clucked because, of course, they'd forgotten, as such women do, that bold and blunt view of yourself, in oily gloopy mass, is too much; even a hard look in the mirror. You want the glamour, not the corpse light or the common. You want the gloss, not the cad and imperfect children. But there are always other parties: a choracle of another day. Signs and visions. If you just never learn. A fondue with the face and force of Tiresias, the blind seer; a dip that goes down deep, deep and up come Dione and Zeus at Epirus.

Sometimes, on bad days, Donna Griffiths puts on the chocolate fountain for herself, laughing, hoping for better.

That kind of woman. Mother. The jarred pickled egg to your smashed avocado on sourdough. And she grows prettier and prettier and more alabaster as she dips her pork scratchings in the viscous, bubbling liquid while all her children thrive.

jar and the girl

A Ball preserving jar, in its original lucent aquamarine
beauty, lay in a flea market in Virginia. It was tucked into a
scruffy area of kitchenalia and vintage aprons, but that pale
beauty was numinous; the jar was the colour of the best sea
glass and Miriam wanted it at once. After that, she bought
them everywhere she could in the South and took them
home, where the littoral light from them simultaneously
warmed and cooled the stone around her kitchen windows.
Or she gave them to friends, who filled them with glass
marbles and treasures – always remembering to set them
in the light, she said, because of the watery sea colour and
the delicacy of the embossed script: *Ball. Perfect Mason*, they
said. The jars made her forget, too. When you bask in colour,
you may push back the horror and what dreams may come,
if only for a slender moment.

But still you push. And then sometimes you must peel, chop, core, boil and simmer.

Because the push does not work.

The jars she had bought, stallholders told her, were from the 1950s and bought from house and farm clearances over the South. What might a Virginian farmer's wife of that time have thought of Miriam's collecting these jars, supposed to be tough and practical and used for preserving? Perhaps what her own mother would have thought, Miriam decided: that if something was practical, one should hardly be noticing its beauty. Mother and Grandmother used to pause before they shut the door of the huge Somerset larder just so that they could admire the big jars of pickled eggs and onions and cabbage and the preserved damsons, apples and plums from the trees in their garden. The satisfaction of good housekeeping. *And yet and yet.* In the warp and weft of that housekeeping was not charity, but parsimony. Competition. And knowing that, in dark vinegar and glowing, bouncing globules, lies something frightening. It wasn't the beauty of the jars, for Grandmother, but the soused contents. In the good housekeeping, a sharp white tooth. An embolus of fear.

And Mother. Just the same. Pride in the bounty of garden and keening branch, but not generosity. Miriam pushed back the memory and looked at the pellucid jars, her eyes drawn to one and a glimmer that was a rash of cold beryl in the aquamarine. There it was.

Ah, yes.

The frightening thing, ah, yes; it need not even be a thing, but a bottled-up thought.

It starts with a shade you're not sure you've seen. Now? From the corner of your eye. Then a whisper and you know, don't you, that your forebears are back with a jostle and a curse. Quickly, the jars are red-misted, then steamed up all white, in a frenzy. Puffy clouds that aren't pretty. And you can smell them, too. Tiny cumulus that don't smell of rain. Old glass jars should hum of good water – of mountain streams, whiff of yellow beach. So, the burned smell is noticeable and commands that you be observant. That's how it was for Miriam now, standing in front of the jars, facing them, willing them to empty, not to smell, to keep clear and free their gorgeous colour from those troubling wisps that were not her.

A cackle. Mother, Grandmother and all the Virginia housewives joined in. You. Silly girl at the stove, burned the cakes; get back into the pantry: there's a deep shelf and *there... there... are the biggest jars, all full of unmentionables you wouldn't believe, oh pickles, honey, pickles, in biiiiig ole jars...*

I will not break my jars. Quick as a flash, Miriam in survival mode, proprioception all wrong, unsure of her edges. Oh, ha ha ha. But not so fast, harridans. See her peel and core and chop and bud up something glowing until it's hot and spicy and bigger, more generous than you all. Sterilise the jars, warm them, fill them with this umber beauty and they do not crack. Miriam. does not crack. She sets her teeth and fills the jars and screws on lids with shaking hands but still it is done. That burning smell is eclipsed, the cumulus that does not smell of rain, the laugh. The red mist is swallowed up by good things and she has survived.

At the top, a sliver of lovely aquamarine, unsullied by the sadness or the rancour that should not be inheritance perpetual. That Ball preserving jar, in its original lucent aquamarine beauty, had lain in a flea market in Virginia.

It was tucked into a scruffy area of kitchenalia and vintage aprons, but that pale beauty was numinous; the jar was the colour of the best sea glass and Miriam had wanted it at once. She collected more and when they came, the laughs and cackles and the *you you yous* she filled these jars up with the good things: *Ball. Perfect Mason.*

And,

Bread and Butter pickles.

Apple chutney.

Miriam, September 2018.

sherbet

You probably know this, but it is possible to construct a belief system around anything. There are those who revere Prince Philip, whose cult revolves around a deity of jettisoned cargo. There are those who pace and faint around Our Lady and those for whom a leg of lamb caparisoning with caper sauce brings forth the gift of tongues. There are acolytes who, replete already in their belief, add to it with a miracle, a tapestry of Jesus that wept, an incorruptible body or the bleeding yew tree of Nevern in our Wales.

And Geraint Llewhellin, born a foot-washing Baptist, had a revelation the first time he tried a sherbet dab and there's no shame in that. He was a grown man, getting on, with a sweet tooth, though not all his teeth, and some black like a rancid badger. And he stopped at the sweetie shop in the village for a half-pound of something in the old language – rhubarb and custards, comfits of some kind – but his eye was caught by a little, pale yellow sleeve and a scant black tongue sticking out of it. The yellow of the paper was soft and beguiling, and he was not a man whose life had been abundant in soft and beguiling things; he stroked it, smelled it. Papery, like old books, bibles for the foot-washers.

'Ah, an excellent choice, Mr. Llewhellin,' said Aeres Williams, the keeper of the shop. 'But I wonder, how you will eat it, bach. Will you gently suck, or will you shovel up with the liquorice, drunk on the acid-carbonate reaction with your own saliva?' She sucked up her drool, reached onto the top shelf and wedged some mint imperials into the spaces where teeth were missing before placing three large American hard gums in the back of her mouth. Geraint had always had an uncomfortable erotic stirring whenever he saw Aeres Williams and it was hard to manage now, wrong money coming forth and change placed into his hands, ushering forth the incongruous words, 'Oh, gently, Aeres,' as he thought of how he might rock her at night, before devouring her, although he had never learned how.

Geraint decided he would concentrate, all alone, on this new sweet he had never tried. Through the village the packet was velvet in his warm trouser pocket, tamping down the uncomfortable erotic stirrings for Aeres. And in a damp parlour, below Jesus and a photograph his late father had taken of the bleeding yew tree out at Nevern in our Wales, he cradled his little blessing and sucked.

Whoosh. Why had he never tried such madness before? It was like a portal into something new as the acid-carbonate reaction, soothed by a gentle wash of icing sugar, lathered across his tongue. It was then, as he swallowed, as his throat warmed, that more sap blood seemed to come from the tree in his father's photograph and that Jesus winked for love of him. And as he sucked he began to gibber and gibe. And did not stop. It was a miracle; this quiet and stifled man *did not stop*. Out into the street he went, uttering the gift of prophecy and, because, quite rightly, madness was accepted and loved, passers-by listened. By noon, Geraint Llewhellin was famous. In the surrounding villages, people knew his name and came to hear his prophecy. Of harvests and love matches; of reassurance and tellings of the happy quietness of the dead and soon to be. When he tired, Aeres would bring him more sherbet from her shop, but, like his high and mint-imperial-toothed priestess, she forbad anyone else from sucking up the sherbet and now she was his, oh acid-carbonate rapture. And that night he cradled his blessing and learned to devour.

The fame of Geraint Llewhellin spread; more sherbet dabs were stockpiled, and a church of sorts was erected, with sherbet in a censer, swinging this way and that, with just a touch of lemon oil for added potency. Aeres Williams was the thurifer – she who carried the sherbet – in a silver thurible, sourced from somewhere, and oh how it fizzed and brought the village and surrounding together. There was not a creed exactly; no holy book – just listening and being reverent and taking guidance from this acid-sweet man and his peppermint seer.

You probably know this, but it is possible to construct a belief system around anything. There are those who revere Prince Philip, whose cult revolves around a deity of jettisoned cargo; there are those who pace and faint around

Our Lady and those for whom a leg of lamb caparisoning with caper sauce brings forth the gift of tongues. There are those who, replete already in their belief, add to it with a miracle, a tapestry of Jesus that wept, an incorruptible body or the bleeding yew tree of Nevern in our Wales. And there are those, quiet and pretty, who sit and listen as acid-carbonate hits an old tongue and when what is said reverberates in the old room and out into the world. And who are comforted by the darkness there, the swing of the thurible filled with sherbet – burning on special days, feast days, to be sure.

bread and salt

In our convivial homeland, when important, respected or admired guests arrive, they are presented with a loaf of bread; we favour that which we call a *korovai*. It is placed on a *rushnyk*, the embroidered ritual cloth. A salt holder or a salt cellar is placed on top of the bread or secured in a hole on the top of the loaf. And on official occasions, the bread and salt are usually presented by fresh young women dressed in national costumes, the *sarafan* and *kokoshnik*, and it is a picture. We love hospitality, here in our quiet town, yes yes. And, say, can you hear it whispering, the conviviality? The graciousness? Can you see the salty moisture on the lips of the young women? *Forgive me*, for I should not speak of such rapacity. But I am an old man now, so old, and my pulse soars quickly when I think of things unguent and well as the desiccant salt and dry bread. And the two together, oh! *But forgive me*. I am also too old.

Now, this bread and salt tradition of which I speak gave rise to the Russian word which expresses a person's hospitality: it is *khlebosolny*, which is to say *bready-salty*. To further my exposition, you should know that the word *bread* is associated in Russian culture with hospitality, because bread is the most respected food; then, the salt is associated with long friendship. We have a saying: 'to eat a pood of salt with someone'. Salt has historically been a prized commodity expensive, much taxed. Do not sprinkle it lightly. Even I, rich beyond your compare, would not dare to do so. Do not misprize it. *Ever*. Not in my presence, dear one. I have many riches and many feasts at my home, though I prefer to lay a fine table and eat much later. Much, much later. And heretically. None of this means I am wasteful or ungrateful of fine commodity.

There also is a traditional Russian greeting: '*Khleb da sol!*' Here – it is so much more elegant to utter in our language, 'Хлеб да соль!' *Ha! Bread and salt!* The phrase is to be uttered by an arriving guest as an expression of good wish towards the host's household. And when I invite you in, stepping over the threshold of my fine home of your own free will, I expect this from you. Хлеб да соль, you know, has often been used by beggars as an implicit hint to be fed. I know well that in the village those supple minds give a mocking rhymed response: '*Khleb da sol! – Yem da svoy!*' Again, for elegance, 'Хлеб да соль! – ем да свой!' Which is to say, 'Bread and salt! – I am eating and it is my own!' Ungenerous! And so, the villagers tell them, poor famished things, to go away with mocks and maws, but an unsuspecting beggar comes instead to my door and I do not mock. He is frail, I feed him, later he will feed me and then, sweet revenant, he may exist in motes of dust, or plumes of smoke. He may take back the mock to the issuers; the mote evolves into a well-fed beggar in front of their swooning eyes. The plumes drift under their bedroom door. So, revenge is taken on the unmannerly. Once, I was hungry too. And always, generations back, before I was *Eretik, toothsome and fixing my evil eye*, I was cultured. Do you think a monster is uncivil?

Now, if you come to my house, 'Хлеб да соль!' *Ha! Bread and salt!* Hospitality. Say it to me, too, as I told before, as a guest respecting his host. Manners are important; they are not trinkets to dispose of when you tire of possession. Bread and salt, we say. And we are friends.

But I will still eat you.

trimalchio jones

(With apologies to the *Satyricon* of Petronius, late first century AD. And to F. Scott Fitzgerald.)

'There was a vision of a Roman feast like that of Trimalchio, with a horror in a covered platter.'

The Rats in the Walls, **H. P. Lovecraft.**

It was the night of the grand feast at the house of Trimalchio Jones. I am a man of some standing and expectation, but modest enough to know I am *a country mile* away from that of our host. And when I have given feasts, well now, I have done my best to extend two courses with pleasant conversation; to make myself raconteur, constrained as I am by pecuniary matters. And all this time, I craved abundance. *Immodesty*. I thought I had it when the much-wanted dinner invitation came from Trimalchio Jones. Oh, the pleasure I felt then!

But now, at his villa, and after some time of anticipation and frustrated small talk, finally we took our places. Boys from Alexandria poured iced water over our hands. Others followed them and attended to our feet, removing any hangnails with great skill. I said, 'Slough at my corns, boys – and bring me wine.' And so, they sloughed and slugged for me. They sang, these pretty boys, and there was one – the corn slougher, as I recall – cooing in a shrill voice while he attended to me, and to anyone else who needed their extremities soothed. It was a particularly musical dinner party. And I was glad to be rid of the hangnails and the bothersome corns. A success! I took an indecent pleasure in watching the efforts of those who served, too; I mean, as I basked in indolence and was hungry.

But I must attend to detail of the feast and of our host, Trimalchio Jones. Yes, this Trimalchio walked into the room at first, but, overcome with lassitude, had his servants carry him to his eating couch. He was fanned, of course, and had, in his hand, that strange green ball he always carries, stretching it across his hand, rolling to his fingertips and back. He throws it up in the air. It is said that he has a superstition: should the ball fall to the floor, some peril would befall. Some extremely elegant hors d'oeuvres were served at this point; by now everyone had taken his place with the exception of Trimalchio, for whom, strangely enough, the place at the top was reserved, yet rejected. I wondered that a man of his standing did not choose to be at the head of the table, but instead to one side and spectating, with some of us craning our necks to do him honour.

The serving dishes were something to behold, for the first course included an ass fashioned from Corinthian bronze and carrying two panniers, white olives on one side and black on the other. *Like the teeth of Trimalchio Jones,* whispered a man, then looked scared. Cradled on the bronze and over the ass were two fine pieces of plate, inscribed with the legend of Trimalchio. And on these plates were roasted dormice sprinkled with honey and poppy seeds. There were burnished sausages, too, and slivers of mutton done up very fine with spices and sprinkled with pomegranate seeds.

And then another laden ass arrived, with sweet apples and dates and more succulent shards of meat, and a hecatomb of other elegant dishes I did not find time to name or sample. I watched Trimalchio himself, reclining on his couch and grazing, bored and sad, sometimes fed shavings of the hors d'oeuvres by his servants and, always, rolling and tossing up the green ball. Each time the ball was suspended in the air, I saw a look of anxiety pass his face: what if the ball could not escape the eventual and ineluctable fall to the marble floor? Was that it? As I said, he was known to be a deeply superstitious man, so what might he have supposed the fall of the green ball would portend? For him, or was it for others?

He caught it, rolled it back towards his wrist and the look passed. He sucked and sucked through his teeth.

A suspiration. *Hehhhhhh.*

Trimalchio Jones sighed and reclined further on his pile of tightly stuffed cushions, azure and peacock in hue. His broad head with tightly cropped white hair stuck out, broad-beamed turtle, from a scarlet coat; around his throat he wore an extraordinary assemblage of napkins, silk, cotton and satin; heliotrope stripes and gentian tassels dangling here and there. He was, himself, a feast of colour. He wore heavy gilt rings and one was studded with little stars; he would push up the sleeves of the expansive scarlet coat to show off his gold armlet and ivory circlets. Yes, a feast, a generous host, but bored, bored, bored. Host of this orgiastic evening and, yet, not partaking, and sad.

Now, he spoke. After picking the dormouse flesh from his teeth with a silver toothpick provided by his minions, he began: 'My friends, I hadn't wanted to come into the dining room yet. But if I stayed away anymore, I would have kept you back, so, look, my guests. I've deprived myself of all my little pleasures for you. *For you*. And now, I am sure you will allow me to finish my game.'

What game?

A boy brought in a large and beautifully carved wooden hen, its wings spread round it the way hens do when they are broody. It sat on a nest of burnished twigs and straw – a phoenix! – and two slaves hurried behind the boy. Then, as the orchestra played, the slaves began searching through the straw and dug out peahens' eggs, which they distributed to the guests. Trimalchio, raising himself slightly from his couch, laughed heartily. 'My friends, I gave orders for that bird to sit on some peahens' eggs. I gave instruction to the hen itself! I hope to goodness they are not starting to hatch. However, let's try them and see if they are still soft.'

We attacked the eggs at his command and found them to be made of rich pastry, filled with rich yellow yolk and, at its heart, not a chick but a plump little figpecker. It was a glorious confection and yet, digging in with a silver spoon, watching Trimalchio paw at his green ball, I felt bilious and my soul ached that I should be a guest. I thought, then, that I alone seemed to feel this way, and Trimalchio Jones caught my eye and a smirk came across that fine face all shrouded in scarlet and amaranth.

He clapped his hands; surely it was too soon after the eggs for the next sumptuous course? Another boy ran in with food at a panic and dropped the salvers. Trimalchio Jones had the boy's ears boxed, got him to clear it up, then told him to throw it down again. A cleaner came in with a broom and began to sweep up the silver plate along with the rest of the rubbish. Trimalchio Jones had more ears boxed and laughed. Two long-haired Ethiopians followed the smarting boys, carrying a fantastic bronze platter of fruits all done up like a mossy garden wall, behind which there was a piece of grassy turf bearing a great honeycomb. A young Egyptian slave carried around bread in a silver oven and the music grew louder.

'Eat, *eat*, my friends. I would be disappointed if you did not.'

Dancers hurtled forward in time to the music and removed the lid of another great dish, revealing underneath plump fowls, sows' udders, and a hare with wings fixed to his middle to look like Pegasus. We saw figures of Marsyas with little skin bottles, which let a peppery fish sauce go running over some fish that seemed to be swimming in a little river, a murky stream; not pretty. The creatures were struggling and choking.

'Applaud my fare. Stand up and applaud, my sweet guests,' he cried. A whip struck at the assemblage of nearby minions. They applauded as if their lives depended on it.

We all joined in the servants' applause and amid some laughter we helped ourselves to these quite exquisite things. Trimalchio was every bit as happy as we were with this sort of trick. 'Carver!' he cried, pointing to the winged hare, which had been followed by further plates of the same. Up came the man with the carving knife and, with his hands moving in time to the orchestra, he sliced up the victuals like a charioteer battling to the sound of organ music. And still Trimalchio went on saying insistently: 'Carver, Carver!' And on and on, flashes of knives.

'Carve, Carver!' And, 'Carver! Carve, carve, carve, *cave, cave, caveat emptor… yes… caveat, cave epulone…* yes carve!' The English had melted into a strange language which I could not understand and, I sensed, might only belong to its speaker.

He spoke again, smiling voice, with no smile on that face.

'Hell drags us off and that is the lot; so, let us live a little space. At least while we can feed our face.' Yes, this is what Trimalchio Jones said, in his rhyme, darkly pat. And he bid us applaud more and then stroke and regard the labels of all the bottles of vintage wine that we had at table.

Another course. Too soon. Tables and guests groaned and the air was hot. Dainties. Chickpeas; beefsteak; testicles and kidneys; fruits. A sow's udder or two; a sea scorpion; a sea bream; lobster and some sweet cheesecakes with a granular fig paste. I will confess it now, that we Romans may favour an heterogenous plate, but here was something sickening, sauced with his self-regard and cajoles that became like threats – and always the pulse and roll and pulse and roll of the green ball of Trimalchio Jones: 'So the starry sky turns round like a millstone, always bringing some trouble, and men being born or dying.' He fingered the ball, his face reddening.

Then the servants came up and laid across the couches embroidered coverlets for us to relax on, and they laid about us all the paraphernalia of hunting and of fishing.

Unsettled, nauseated from such excessive and conspicuous consumption, now tears came forth from the banqueters and an egregious laughter as Spartan hounds began dashing everywhere, even round the table. Behind them came more of the Ethiopian servers with a great dish and on it lay a wild boar of the largest possible size; from its tusks dangled two baskets woven from palm leaves, one full of fresh Syrian dates, the other of dried Theban dates. Little piglets made of cake were all round it, as though at its dugs, suggesting it was a brood sow being served. Now a man came forward tentatively, pushed by the foot of Trimalchio Jones. 'Kill the boar!' our host shouted and the man struck at the flanks with his sword; out flew a flock of thrushes. Screaming, panicked birds, not a pretty soaring. And the Spartan hounds bayed and snapped; the bird pecked and the hounds screeched and whimpered.

The room was a whirligig of dogs and birds and men and sunburned delicacies on bronze platters. Above it all boomed the bigger voice: 'Let us begin our feast again. I, I will not eat. I was sated, long ago.'

We heard bolts slide on doors and a hollow laugh from our host. Now, the boys from Alexandria poured iced water over our hands. Others followed them and attended to our feet, promising that they would remove any hangnails with great skill. I said, 'That you did already!' 'What of your fingernails, my lord,' they laughed. 'Or the fusty hair on your ears and in your nostrils?' And I thwacked at them for their impertinence. But determinedly they sloughed and slugged at my hands and a boy took burning leaves and a puff of burning linen with perfumed oils on it and singed the hair on my ears: I smelled like roasted meat, dead and aromatic. They sang, these pretty boys, and there was one – the corn slougher, as I recall – cooing in a shrill voice while he attended to me – and anyone else who needed their extremities soothed. It was a particularly musical dinner party. And I suppose I was glad to be rid of the fusty hair and the jagged nails.

A suspiration. *Hehhhhhh.*

On the couch, Trimalchio Jones seemed to have roused from his lassitude. His eyes were glittering in his head and they were of the darkest colour: like aphotic pools. 'Eat!' he cried as the feast began again. He rolled the ball towards his wrist and down again, and threw: the anxiety passed across that evil face – and now I saw that this was what it was – and then he settled and smiled. Until he dropped that ball upon the floor and the feast was stayed, until the ineluctable fall occurred, here we would remain, as a guest of Trimalchio Jones. Yet an ineluctable fall may not be imminent; time is large, like a grand feast. And so we eat, are sloughed and watered, and wait.

Breaking our hearts and full.

A suspiration. *Hehhhhhh. A black tooth. An ivory circlet. Aphotic eye and a long dark nail basking on a scarlet coat.*

sweetie

Oh, how lovely. Frangipane, stardust, cold magic sherbet and a slurp of something blue.

At some point in the past, every village in our country had a little shop, and the little shop was where sweetie lived. There they were, the past children and the bigger past people. The doorbell *ting*ed behind them. Hear it, now? Above the clamour of your rent heart? Those past children could see straight through to the post office counter where Mrs. Thomas was serving the next customer with penny stamps and his pension. And every week, she short-changed him, and the past children laughed.

It was slow-moving, slow-speaking Miss Llewhellin of the rat teeth who came forward to serve them. They could take their time with her as they weighed the merits of humbugs against liquorice allsorts, or Nuttall's mintoes against dolly mixtures. These shelves, with thirty-six big glass bottles to inspect and choose from. Oh, pleasure and pleasure and rot! The bottles winked cheerfully at them in the soft, mellow afternoon sunlight, seeming to say, 'Choose me. Choose me.' Miss Llewhellin whispered it too, through her rat teeth and tears: 'Choose me…' And the bottles winked and, if you ever pressed your ear up hard to the big glass bottles, you'd have heard a thin, dry voice rasping, 'Sweetie… sweetie… sweetie.' But whether the big glass bottles spoke, or whether it was Miss Llewhellin of the rat teeth trying to frighten the past children, or whether there, on the broad shelves, sat something entirely different, embolus eternal-candied and horrid, well now, I cannot say.

What else could the past children see? Aniseed balls, with a sweet, powdery bloom on them, were in one jar; the pink pastel colours of fruit drops were in the next. The rich brown sheen of Sharpes' Blue Bird toffee pieces were next to the brindle and white whirls of Maynards' delights. Lovely they were, but they gave you toothache if they took out one of your fillings. All you would get then was iodine treatment to see you through to the next visit of the school dentist, months away. Or you could just say, 'To hell with it,' and let them all fall out and live, thereafter, off lovers and marshmallows. There were plenty of toothless people in the village, though the lovers were shared, for being thin on the ground. But back to the sweeties. Small black rolls of liquorice gleamed dully; sherbet lemons spoke of blazing summer (before summer was too hot) and Fox's Glacier mints of the North Pole, looking to the past children like bits chipped from an ice flow, when the ice flows weren't breaking off of their own accord. In *those* days. The before days.

Don't you see the flamingo and white mint shrimps, liquorice comfits, rhubarb and custard, fruit pastilles; left over from Christmas-time, a box of sugared almonds that Father Christmas had failed to deliver to a child, hopeless and praying for grace? Or a husband to a wife craving that lambent smoothness, the thinness of the sugar shell upon that crisp nut. Or the girl nobody wanted, dressed in brown or watery grey, wishing for the allure of the pretty pastel sweet in a world of mud and sad. Or to Miss Llewhellin of the rat teeth who had never known a man, though she had seen plenty.

The past children browsed and bought and sucked and then that time was away. And Miss Llewhellin of the rat teeth keened and died. The little shop was shuffled off, but to this day its wreckage resides there in the now world. And still a thin dry voice rasping, 'Sweetie… sweetie… sweetie.'

notes on the text

'Cave Venus et Stellas' and 'Feasting; Fasting' were first published in *The Shadow Booth: Vol 2*, ed. Dan Coxon, 2018; 'Shadow Babies' Supper' is adapted from an earlier memoir piece published on the web version of *The Shadow Booth*. 'Trimalchio Jones' makes use of some text from the *Satyricon* of Petronius, c. first century AD and is also inspired, in turn, by F. Scott Fitzgerald's *The Great Gatsby*, the original title of which was 'Trimalchio in West Egg'.

acknowledgements

Thank you thank you to Influx Press and especially to Gary Budden who took on this peculiar book and worked with me on it. Thank you to Sanya and Kit at Influx. To my agent Kate Johnson of Mackenzie Wolf Literary in New York. To my extended family and my very dear friends, live and undead – in short, to my tribe – you know who you are. To the horrors that made my imagination what it is: more of this book is true than you might imagine.

This book is, as ever, for Ned, Elijah, Isaac and Caleb. My heart goes with you. X

about the author

Anna Vaught is a novelist, poet, essayist, reviewer, and editor. She is also a secondary English teacher, tutor and mentor to young people, mental health campaigner and advocate, volunteer and mum to a large brood. She is the author of numerous books, including the novel *Saving Lucia* (Bluemoose). Her work has appeared in *Best British Horror*, *Litro*, *The Shadow Booth*, *Review 31* and many more. You can find her on Twitter @bookwormvaught and www.annavaughtwrites.com.

Influx Press is an independent publisher based in London, committed to publishing innovative and challenging literature from across the UK and beyond.

Lifetime supporters: Bob West and Barbara Richards

www.influxpress.com
@Influxpress

EXERCISES IN CONTROL
Annabel Banks

'Compelling, weird and funny slices of fiction served by a daring new writer.'
— *i-D*

'A debut collection about the human obsession with control. No matter how normal the opening scenario, each of these stories ends in the strangest place.'
— *New Scientist*

'Consistently dark, surprising and playful... a cohesive and compulsively readable collection..'
— *Mslexia*

A lonely woman invites danger between tedious dates; a station guard plays a bloody game of heads-or-tails; an office cleaner sneaks into a forbidden room hiding grim secrets.

Compelling and provocative, Annabel Banks's debut short fiction collection draws deeply upon the human need to be in control — no matter how devastating the cost.

ISBN: 9781910312476

THIS WAY TO DEPARTURES
Linda Mannheim

'Mannheim compassionately conveys the injustices of poverty.'
— *Guardian*

'There's anger, righteous indignation and sorrow in these stories, relatable characters and situations and solid connections with the real world that belie its theme of dislocation.'
— *The Herald*

What happens when we leave the places we're from? What do we lose, and who do we become, and what parts of our pasts are unshakeable?

Linda Mannheim's second short story collection focuses on people who have relocated – both voluntarily and involuntarily.

Opening with Miami-set political thriller, 'Noir', this exquisitely rendered set of stories will leave you reeling.

This Way to Departures is a deeply affecting portrait of American society and the constant search for a place to call 'home'.

ISBN: 9781910312438

HOW THE LIGHT GETS IN

Clare Fisher

'Cements her position as an innovative literary talent.'
— *New Statesman*

'Fisher's tales are funny and moving, and you'll treasure them all.'
— *Stylist*

'If fiction was a language, Clare Fisher would be one of its native speakers: a writer whose whole response to the world is brilliantly story-shaped.'
— Francis Spufford, author of *Golden Hill*

How The Light Gets In is the first collection from award winning short story writer and novelist, Clare Fisher. A book of very short stories that explores the spaces between light and dark and how we find our way from one to the other.

From buffering Skype chats and the truth about beards, to fried chicken shops and the things smartphones make you less likely to do when alone in a public place, Fisher paints a complex, funny and moving portrait of contemporary British life.

ISBN: 9781910312124